Publisher's Cataloging-in-Publication
(Provided by Quality Books, Inc.)

Quintero-Spongberg, Emily, 1948-
     Hannibal and the king / Emily Quintero-Spongberg;
   illustrated by Tim Spongberg, -- 1st ed.
     p. cm.
          SUMMARY: On the day of Jesus' entry into Jerusalem, the animals in a stable discuss and argue about which one of them will be chosen to carry him.
          ISBN: 1-893659-00-3

          1. Bible stories, English--N.T. Gospels. 2. Animals--Juvenile fiction. 3. Jesus Christ--Entry into Jerusalem--Juvenile fiction. 4. Donkeys--Juvenile fiction.

          I. Spongberg, Timothy, 1949-
          II. Title

                             [Fic]
PZ7.Q425Han 1999   QBI99-242

"Hi! I'm Hannibal. Would you like to meet my friends?"

For my wonderful children, Annette, Sandie, Gabriel, and Allison, who inspire me with their love and friendship. And to my two beautiful granddaughters, Emily and E'lin, who keep me young.

To my tremendously talented husband, Tim, who encouraged me to take on this project. This book would not have been possible without his support and his endless hours of work.

A special thanks to Patricia Reilly Giff, who shares her knowledge so graciously and generously with her student authors. And for her continual encouragement.

   E.S.

To my wife, Emily, whose striving for perfection has inspired me to explore another facet of my art.

   T.S.

Hannibal
and the
KING

by **Emily Quintero-Spongberg**

illustrated by **Tim Spongberg**

Rainbow House Publishing
Bridgeport, Connecticut

Morning had fallen on the modest stable in the small town just outside of Jerusalem. The sun crept through the tiny windows, announcing the new day. Its light filtered through the cracks of the aging roof, creating an aura of light that brightened and cheered its humble surroundings. The smell of fresh hay was in the air, and the animals rose from their sleep to its sweet aroma, making their way to the troughs.

Soon after, excitement filled the stable as the animals scampered around in a bustle over the arrival of a kindly stranger.

"What's all the commotion about, Barnaby?" asked Hannibal the gray donkey, who was also the youngest animal in the stable.

"Haven't you heard?" said Barnaby, the one-humped brown camel. "Our stable has been selected. A man named Peter is here to pick one of us to bring Jesus into Jerusalem. Can you imagine, Hannibal? One of us will carry the King of Kings."

"Has he chosen anyone yet?" Hannibal asked.

"No, not yet, but we all want to be the one. Don't you?" Barnaby asked.

"O-o-o-h, no! I couldn't," said Hannibal with a trembling voice. "I'm too young and my hair isn't full-grown yet. It's a bit scraggly. My legs aren't very steady and I don't know how far I could go. I've never carried anyone on my back before. Besides," Hannibal sighed as he lowered his head, "Jesus is the Son of God. I'm sure they will want the strongest and most beautiful beast in the stable."

"Move out of my way. Let me through," said the enormous black horse with a deep voice that matched his size. "I think I should be the one," he said as he stomped on the stable floor. "I am strong, courageous, and beautiful," he bragged, "and I certainly have the strongest back in the stable. I will carry him gently. After all, He's a king, and kings ride horses. Everyone knows that!"

"L-e-e-e-t me in! I want him to pick me," said the brawny white mule, wiggling her way through. " You might be strong and beautiful, but what about my strong back? I have carried some very important people. I too am muscular and light-footed. If this man Peter knows anything at all about mules, he'll pick me," she declared as she plowed through the stable, shoving those in her way.

"Well, I don't like to brag," interrupted Barnaby the camel, "but I have been known to carry many rich and important people myself, and I can carry heavy loads and go days without water. You wait and see. Peter will pick me," he said, his nostrils flaring and his head tilted high in the air.

One by one, the animals displayed their fine qualities. They all tried to convince each other why they should be chosen.

At that moment, the stable keeper came in and began to line up the animals so that the visitor would be able to choose the best of the herd. He lined them up from the strongest and largest to the smallest.

"Well!" said the stable keeper, bewildered by the size of his herd. "I didn't realize there were so many of you. I'll have to narrow down my selection. I will choose one more."

Hannibal and Barnaby were at the far end of the stable, hoping to be chosen by the stable keeper.

"Did you hear what he said, Hannibal? He's only going to pick one more, and you are ahead of me. I'll never get chosen!" yelled Barnaby frantically. "I would have carried Him so gently and carefully," he muttered.

Hannibal felt bad for Barnaby. After all, Barnaby was his best friend. What could he do?

Just then the stable keeper approached them. He was walking straight toward Hannibal.

"Barnaby, take my place," hollered Hannibal, fidgeting to get out of the way and in the back of the line. "This is your only chance. Hurry!"

Barnaby practically knocked Hannibal over as he plunged to the front so he could be chosen by the stable keeper. His head up in the air, he arrogantly showed off his height and strength as the stable keeper led him away to be placed in the line with the other animals he had chosen. He didn't even look back to thank Hannibal for his thoughtfulness and for allowing him to take his place.

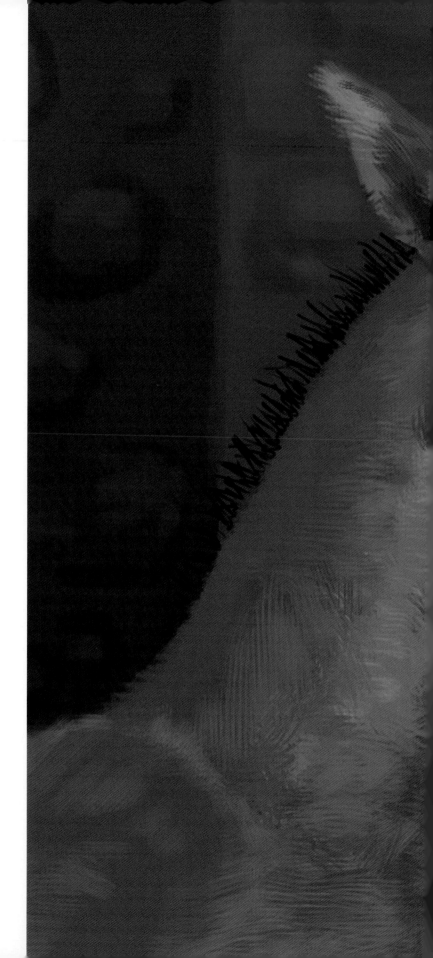

Hannibal pulled away from the others and huddled himself in a corner of the stable with his mother, Moriah.

Moriah was the very donkey that carried Mary, the mother of Jesus, into Bethlehem. That's the place where Jesus was born. She also lived with them in Nazareth for many years. When Jesus left home, Mary gave her to a friend who was a stable keeper.

Shortly after, the stable keeper led
Peter to the animals he had chosen for
him. Peter walked through the stable
looking at the animals, sometimes
pausing to stroke them gently and talk
with them. He liked the animals and
appreciated their hard work.

"Are these all the beasts you have?"
Peter asked the stable keeper. This is a
fine herd but they are not what I am
looking for." Peter said. "I am looking
for two special beasts, one will carry
the Master and the other will follow
along."

"Well, I do have two more, Sir." The
stable keeper led Peter to the back of
the stable.

"Here they are," said the stable keeper. "As you can see, she's too old and he's too young. He's never been ridden."

"Hum!" Peter looked over the little donkey, putting a hand under his chin. He leaned over toward Hannibal and lovingly stroked his back and legs.

Peter saw that Hannibal was a humble donkey who would carry Jesus with gentleness and great care.

"Jesus sent me to find two beasts for Him, and He said I would find them here. I am certain they are the animals I was sent here for," Peter said.

"Well, then," Peter said happily, "I'll take him and his mother. He'll carry the Master into Jerusalem." And with a smile, Peter led Hannibal and Moriah away.

"Prepare them and we'll be on our way."

The stable keeper, scratching his head in confusion over Peter's choice, set out to brush them and prepare them for their journey. He returned shortly with both of the donkeys.

"What are their names?" Peter asked.

"She's called Moriah," said the stable keeper. "A fine beast in her younger days, and the young one is her son, Hannibal."

Peter turned to Hannibal and said, "Hannibal, you have a busy and exciting day ahead of you. Tomorrow, you will carry Jesus into Jerusalem."

The other animals couldn't believe that Peter had chosen Hannibal over them.

"Why, he's too young, an ordinary donkey. He's never carried anyone before," they said. "How could this man Peter pass up our magnificence and strength over this untrained donkey colt?"

A new day proclaimed its arrival. The moon had gone to sleep, and the sun was again shining and giving its warm glow to the sleepy town, where Jesus and his friends were staying.

"Why, Moriah, how good to see you after all these years," Jesus said with a smile. "You have kept yourself well. I have missed you, my friend!" Jesus exclaimed as he stroked her back and tickled her behind the ears. "I remember the happy times we had together, you and I."

How wonderful it felt. Moriah remembered the gentle-hearted little boy from Nazareth who many years ago had taken care of her and been her friend.

"Moriah, today your son will carry me into Jerusalem." Jesus smiled at Hannibal and softly stroked his back.

"I know you gave up your place in line, Hannibal," Jesus said warmly, "you are a good friend."

Moriah beamed with joy. Her son had been chosen to ride Jesus, just as she had so many years ago.

Jesus carefully mounted the donkey. "Well, Hannibal, this is a very special day for both of us."

Hannibal was so happy, and so proud to have Jesus on his back, he glowed. He felt strong and beautiful.

When they got to Jerusalem the people were waving branches and shouting, "Hosanna! Hosanna! Jesus is King!" They were throwing their coats on the ground so that Hannibal could walk over them. After all, he was carrying the King of Kings.